I0596720

Claim It

WHEN DISASTER STRIKES, WILL YOU BE READY?
Michael The Adjuster

*Disclaimer - All individual names and business names are fictional. Situations are based on true events, but not one individual(s) or company(s). Individual claim results may vary. Consult with your insurer on policy definitions, endorsements and exclusions for a clear understanding of your personal situation.

This book goes out to the homeowners navigating claims right now:
Your perseverance is the reason this book exists.
And to every homeowner who's ever had to fight for fairness:
Your story deserves to be heard.

This one was written for you.

TABLE OF CONTENTS

Before the Water Comes

When you're buying a home there is bound to be some mention of homeowners' insurance. You'll even see advertisements on tv and on the radio that it's cheaper to bundle your home and auto insurance. However, no one really talks about what it's like to use it, when it can be used or how you should navigate using it. No one ever anticipates using their insurance, more importantly, most people don't even know they can use it for several things.

A home comes with many things, birthday parties, quiet mornings, and weekend projects. No one pictures leaks, broken shingles, or warped hardwood floors. You certainly don't imagine standing in your living room, ankle-deep in water, wondering what to do next.

But for many homeowners, that moment comes — suddenly, uninvited, and unwanted.

This book is for those moments.

It's designed to guide you through what happens after unexpected damage occurs, told through the true-to-life journey of a woman named Emily — a homeowner just like you, who returned from vacation to find her home damaged by a leaking toilet.

As her story unfolds, you'll see the process behind a homeowners' insurance claim. Of course there are differences in every claim but you'll be better equipped to handle your own claim through Emily's processing. But first;

What Is a Homeowners Insurance Claim?

A homeowners insurance claim is **a formal request to your insurance company for help repairing or replacing something damaged in your home**. It's how your policy turns from just another bill to something actionable.

When things go wrong, this is the system built to help you recover.

But it's more than just filling out a form.

It's a multi-step process involving several professionals, inspections, documents, and decisions — and most importantly, your participation.

Let's break it down and explore the very basics.

The 5 W's of a Homeowners Insurance Claim

Who is involved?

The insurance company, who provides the policy and makes coverage decisions based on the intricacies of those policies.

You, the homeowner, who experiences the loss and files the claim.

The adjusters — both field (who visit your home) and desk (who process the claim). With some companies the desk adjuster can also be the one to inspect.

Contractors or **mitigation teams** who handle cleaning and repairs.

Sometimes, a **third-party inspector** or **engineer**, depending on the type of loss.

What happens during a claim?

You report the damage (often online or by phone).

Two adjusters are assigned (your field and desk adjuster).

You may need to hire emergency cleanup services (i.e. mitigation companies).

Your home is inspected to verify the damage you reported.

The adjuster creates a report which includes a narrative of the damage, photos, measurements, and estimates.

The insurance company reviews the report and determines payment based on the intricacies of your policy limits.

You coordinate repairs — either with your own contractor or someone referred to you by the insurance company.

When should you file a claim?

As soon as you discover damage.

Waiting too long can delay the process or result in denied coverage. (Prolonged damage is not always covered. Insurance mainly addresses sudden losses. There are some exceptions of course.)

Small issues (like a cracked tile or minor leak) may not require a claim — but always document and ask. (You may inquire about your deductible in case you feel like you can cover the cost on your own without the help of the insurance company.)

Where does it take place?

On the phone or online — with the claims department.

In your home — through inspections and repairs.

Inside the "file" — the digital record where every estimate, photo, and note lives.

In your own personal file keeping strategy. Keep records of all correspondence for reference later. The insurance company does this and so should you. This will help in case any damages are found during the repair process and additional funds are to be requested by the insurance company to address those damages.

Why is it important to understand the process?

Because **you are your own best advocate**.

Because every policy has limitations and exclusions.

Because repairs are easier when you know what to expect — and what questions to ask.

This Book Will Walk With You

Throughout Emily's story, you'll see how a single water leak can turn into a full-blown disaster — and how she navigates her insurance claim with the help of professionals, persistence, and patience.

Each chapter will reflect a real step in the claims process: from the moment she finds the damage to the day of her final contractor work through.

You'll also find key notes and tips to help you in your own journey — whether your loss is large, small, or somewhere in between.

This isn't just a story.

It's a survival manual in disguise.

INTRODUCTION

How to Read This Book

This is a story of a new homeowner and her first encounter with filing an insurance claim.

Emily Carter's journey through her home insurance claim is designed to feel real — because it *is* real.

Every challenge, every mistake, every small victory she experiences is pulled directly from real-world insurance claims.

You will learn:
- How claims are **really** filed (and how they sometimes go wrong).
- What mitigation and rebuild crews do — and what they sometimes forget.
- How insurance payments are calculated, delayed, and negotiated.
- How to spot the red flags that can cost homeowners thousands of dollars.
- How to finish a claim strongly, with money still in your pocket or at least without overspending.

The key notes listed in each chapter are designed to help you as the homeowner navigate your own claim and advise on some things you may not have considered when filing one. Turn Emily's experience into your own personal advantage.

Whether you're a first-time homeowner, a veteran property investor, or someone who simply wants to be ready *before* a disaster strikes, this book is for you.

By the time you turn the last page, you won't just hope you can handle a claim — **You'll be confident you can.**

Let's get started.

PROLOGUE

Emily Carter

was a young professional. She worked hard and pushed herself to reach one of her main goals in life, home ownership. It had been a rough road, but she was ecstatic she had finally had the opportunity.

After a year of careful budgeting, she was finally able to schedule a nice two-week vacation to Mexico. The day arrived for her departure. She went through a final checklist.

IDs, check.
Dresses, check.
Sun hat, check.

Underwear for a 30-day trip even though it's only 2 weeks, check.
All seemed to be right. She grabbed her bags and headed to the door. Her uber was 2 minutes away. She took a long look at her home. Her most prized possession.

"I'll miss you, but I'll be back soon." A large smile across her face.
The uber arrived, she greeted the driver and put her luggage in the trunk.
It was all smiles as she headed to the airport.

Little did she know what she would return home to.

CHAPTER 1

Coming Home to Disaster

When Emily Carter locked her front door and wheeled her suitcase toward her uber two weeks ago, her biggest worry had been whether she packed enough sunscreen. Mexico had been everything she hoped for: sun-drenched days, ocean breezes, and a blissful escape from the stress of everyday work.

What she wasn't prepared for was the river she found in her living room when she returned.

Emily pushed the door open and froze.

At first, it didn't register.

There was a faint smell of mildew. Sounds of a soft squish beneath her sandals. Warped planks of her hardwood floor, curling up at the edges like the pages of an old book.

And then she looked up.

A dark brown stain blossomed across the ceiling, water still dripping steadily. The dripping matched the sound of a ticking clock nearby, as it reached the soaked carpet below.

Her heart hammered.
Where do you even begin when your home is falling apart?

Instinctively, Emily reached for her phone. The first call she made was to her dad. The moment he picked up the phone the levies to her emotion were broken.

"Daddy, my home is flooded. The whole thing. It's ruined."

Her father attempted to calm her. After a moment, she begins to wipe her tears at his words of solace and encouragement.

"If the water is on the ceiling you gotta check the bathrooms. Before you head to them, check the main water line, you'll need to shut that off to prevent more water damage. Then head to the bathrooms and look for any evidence of leaking pipes.", he said with a calm stern voice.

She tossed her bag aside and rushed to the basement main water shutoff valve. One twist and it was off.

The water damage was catastrophic. It was as if a rainstorm formed in her home. Her once-cozy living room now smelled of rot. She searched the first bathroom. Nothing out of order. She headed to the next one. This one was the culprit. The bathroom floor had an ominous puddle. Emily took a breath.

"Dad, I think I found it.", the words were trembling as she spoke.

She checked under the sink. No damage to these pipes. She checked the shower. No wet areas around the faucet and the showerhead. Then she checked the toilet.

This was it. Her moment of truth. She checked around it then saw there was a crack in the supply line.

"Honey, what was it?"

"It was the supply line. It's cracked."

"I had a feeling it might be something like that. A little thing can cause a lot of damage when unattended."

"What do I do now?"

"First you need to call your insurance. If the damage is as bad as you've described, it's best you get them involved."

Emily shifted through her phone to find her insurance carrier's app. She opened it and scrolled through the options. Buried in the options was a red button: **File a Claim**.

She hesitated.

"Dad, I'm gonna call you back. I need a few minutes to think and prepare to fill this thing out."

"Sweetheart, take as much time as you need. If you need help call me. I'll be over as soon as I can. I love you."

"I love you too.", she says before she hangs up.

What if I say the wrong thing? What if they deny me? They can't deny me, right? It's not my fault this happened.

These thoughts plagued the back of her mind before she finally pressed it.

The form asked simple but critical questions:

- **Date and time of loss:** She entered today's date, guessing the leak started days earlier but noted the date of discovery as when she found the damage.

- **Type of damage:** There was a scroll down menu to choose from. A range of options were listed. Wind, Hail, Water, Fire, Vandalism, Other. She selected "Water."

- **Cause of Loss (if known):** She typed carefully: "A leaking supply line to the upstairs toilet."

- **Is the damage ongoing?** She selected "No," now that the water was shut off.

- **Have emergency services been performed?** "No" - not yet at least.

- **Upload photos:** She snapped close-ups of damaged areas, and a quick video walking through the house narrating what she saw.

The app urged her to **mitigate further damage immediately** but warned her not to make permanent repairs until after an adjuster inspected the property.

Next, she was routed to a live agent. Within minutes, her phone rang.

"Hi Emily, my name is Marissa Thompson. I'm so sorry you're going through this. I'll be handling your claim," the representative said warmly. "Can you walk me through what happened?"

Emily described returning home to find extensive water damage, the dripping ceilings, the warped floors and the damaged contents (i.e., tables, chairs, couches, rugs, tech, etc.).

Marissa asked a few precise follow-up questions:
- **When was the last time the home was occupied?**
- **Have you contacted a plumber yet?**
- **Have you stopped the leak?**
- **Is the property safe to stay in?**

Emily answered carefully, sticking to what she knew. She avoided speculating about hidden damage or repair costs. She's not a contractor after all and was afraid she would say the wrong thing.

"Okay," Marissa said after a pause, "We're opening a new claim under policy number 3471X-65D. Your claim number will be 2224817. Here's what happens next:"

- A licensed **field adjuster** would contact Emily within 24 hours to schedule an inspection.

- Emily should arrange **emergency water mitigation** — removing standing water, drying affected areas — using a vendor of her choice or one the insurance company recommended. The mitigation work was included in her policy (This is not the case for every policy). A recommendation of a company the carrier usually works with was provided.

- **Temporary repairs** to prevent additional damage (like boarding broken windows or shutting off water) were allowed and expected.

- **Permanent repairs** — like replacing drywall or flooring — should wait until after inspection this wat proper evaluation of the loss can be done.

- If Emily needed to relocate because of unsafe living conditions, **additional living expenses** coverage could pay for hotel stays. She should keep all receipts for the stay and food expenses.

Marissa confirmed Emily's email address and sent her a **claim acknowledgment letter** summarizing the conversation, including a claim number, a list of immediate action steps, and her contact information. She should also receive some documentation notating her claim via snail mail in a few days as well.

Before ending the call, Marissa emphasized:

"Document everything. Keep copies of invoices. Take lots of photos before, during, and after any work. And if you have any questions, call me before proceeding. We will do our best to get you back to your home as soon as possible"

Emily hung up feeling slightly steadier — but only slightly. She knew that there was a long road ahead.

She opened a new note in her phone titled **"Claim Log"** and wrote the date, time, and notes from the call.

She called her dad and let him know about the call. He assured her that he would help as much as possible, but organization could make or break her claim.

CHAPTER 2

Meeting the Adjuster

The next day, Emily received a call from an adjuster.

"Hello. My name is Ryan Singer, and I am the field adjuster for an Emily Carter. Does she happen to be available?", a calm tone behind the question.

"Yes, yes. Hi Ryan, this is she."

"Oh great. How are you? Sorry in advance for your loss."

"Thanks. I'm still dealing with the emotions that come with this but I'm ready to start moving."

"That's good to hear. I'll do my best to make this as smooth as possible. First things first, when's a good time for us to meet so we can inspect the damages you reported."

"Honestly, the sooner the better. I can even do as early as tomorrow if you have the time."

"Actually, tomorrow is great. I'll put you for, 9am?"

"Sounds good."

"Great. If you have any documentation or photos, please bring it with you. The more information I can get the better I can fully understand the extent of the damage. Do you happen to have a contractor or plumber that will be at the inspection?"

"No," a sense of worry in rang when she spoke. "Did I need one?"

"No it isn't necessary right away. I always ask because sometimes people have one and they want them present during the initial inspection. I always recommend you get a contractor to assess the damage as well because they can provide an estimate to the insurance company for what they think the repair costs should be."

"Oh okay."

"Yea. No worries. I'll explain what the claims process looks like during our inspection. Did you have any questions for me before our meeting tomorrow?

"Not yet. I'm sure I'll have some tomorrow though."

"No problem. Bring your questions and I'll answer to the best of my ability. I'll see you tomorrow."

"See you then."

The next morning, Emily stood by the front window, peeking nervously through the blinds.

A white SUV pulled into her driveway. The door opened and out stepped a man in khakis and a navy polo. He waved to the front of the home before reaching back in the car to grab his tablet and tool belt. The belt was adorned with a tape measure, a flashlight, a laser measuring device, some post-it notes and a pen.

Emily went to the front door. Before opening the door, she smoothed her hair and wiped her sweaty palms on her pants. This was a first-time experience, and she was nervous about saying anything that would deter a positive resolution for this claim.

After a deep breath, she opened the door.

"Hi, you must be Emily," he said, offering a firm handshake. "I'm Ryan, we spoke on the phone. I'll be inspecting the damage today."

"Yes. Hello. Come in."

Emily welcomed Ryan inside, suddenly self-conscious about the smell — that wet, sour odor of soaked drywall, fabric and wood. Ryan didn't appear fazed.

Must not have been his first rodeo, she thought.

Ryan pulled out his tablet and began to speak.

"Before we get started," Ryan said, "I'll explain the process. When you file a claim, you'll get two adjusters. The first one you'll communicate with is your desk adjuster. This person, in your case Marissa, is the one who makes the final determination of the approval or denial of your claim and will issue a payment if there is one. I, as the field adjuster, am here to take statements, document the damage and take any documentation you may have that relates to the claim. This could be a contractor estimate, paid invoices, or receipts for having to be out of your home. I'll also take photos and measurements of all the damaged areas to provide the insurance company with an estimate of how much I think it would cost to repair. The estimate is created from a software that provides pricing, so I can't tell you how much it would cost off the top of my head. After the inspection I'll write up a report, an estimate and submit all the documentation.

Later, I'll write a report, upload your documentation and submit it to the claims department for the final evaluation by Marissa."

He smiled, but Emily noticed the way he emphasized **"approval or denial."**

Ryan asked if she had any questions, but with all the information she just received none came out.

"Please take your time if you don't have any questions right away." Ryan noticed her hesitance. "For now, if you can show me the cause of the damage and all rooms it has affected that would be great. Also, please walk me through what happened to the best of your ability."

Emily stuck to the facts:
"I came home yesterday evening after being away for about two weeks. I noticed water dripping from the ceiling, the floors were buckled, and there were wet areas all throughout the home. I shut off the water main as soon as I could to prevent further damage."

Ryan nodded, tapping notes into his tablet.

"Have you started making any calls to mitigation companies or contractors?," he asked, still taking notes.

"Not yet. I just followed Maria's instructions on taking pictures. I haven't removed anything or called around for repairs."

Emily ushered Ryan through each of the rooms starting with the bathroom that had the broken pipe and leading through all the affected areas.

Once this initial walkthrough was completed Ryan spoke up.

"Thanks for the walk through. Now I'll be going back to each and begin taking measurements and pictures. Since I know all the areas you can accompany while I do this part if you like. Although, when I do take the pictures I will have to ask you to step out of the room for me to get those overviews."

"Because it's my first claim I'd like to be present as much as possible."

"No problem. If you have questions while I work please do ask but if you can wait till I'm done with the specific room we're in that would be great. I want to make sure I don't miss anything."

"Sure."

Ryan moved room by room. He pointed his tablet at the water-stained ceiling, the warped floorboards, and the bubbling drywall. He snapped dozens of photos from wide angles and close-ups, even photographing things that didn't look damaged.

"Why are you taking pictures of the whole room?" Emily asked.

"The insurance company wants a full picture of both damaged and non-damaged areas. This is to document both the damaged and non-damage present during my initial inspection," he explained. "If something wasn't damaged but gets damaged later, we need to know whether it's related."

As he worked, Ryan explained what he was looking for:

- Signs of long-term leaks (which might not be covered) vs. sudden and accidental damage (which typically is).
- Areas where mold had started forming (often limited or excluded under standard policies).
- Potential structural issues needing immediate attention.

Emily stayed close but gave him space. She wrote down notes on her phone:

- "Water staining is the most severe in the kitchen ceiling."
- "Possible mold in upstairs bathroom wall — ask about coverage."
- "Warped subfloor upstairs?"

After nearly two hours of documenting damage from the second floor to the basement, Ryan wrapped up.

"Now that my inspection has been completed, there's a few things that will happen next. First, you'll need to call that mitigation company immediately because we want to get the wet stuff removed and dry out what can be saved asap. I'll be writing my report over the next 24–48 hours," Ryan explained. "It'll include a photo set, a room-by-room scope, and a line-item estimate."

Emily blinked slowly. "That's... a lot."

"I understand it can feel overwhelming," Ryan said gently. "What I can do is make sure the report I submit reflects the full scope of visible and measurable damage. If anything's borderline, I'll flag it for further review. That gives your desk adjuster more data to make decisions with. I'll also note for Marissa, that mitigation will be coming in and will have more insight into the unseen damage. This'll trigger a flag that there may be some more work needed on the file. Mitigation usually takes a few days, so you'll likely be presented with an estimate before they complete their reports."

Emily crossed her arms, nodding. "And that's where they approve or deny parts of it?"

"Correct," Ryan said. "Your deductible is also applied in that estimate so you're not paying anyone that. Instead, an example would be if someone were to receive $10,000.00 as their approved estimate and their deductible is $1,000.00 they will only receive a check for $9,000.00."

"Okay," she said. "What happens if the mitigation company or my contractor disagrees with your estimate?"

"They can request revisions," Ryan said. "Sometimes they'll send me back out to reinspect and verify the additional claims. What's very important in this process is the contractor must give an estimate which outlines all the damage, materials cost for repair and labor costs separately. This'll give the insurance company all the information they need to make a coverage decision. If I have to reinspect, Marissa will contact me, and we can coordinate a date and time."

He handed her a card.

"I know this is a lot of information to process at once, feel free to contact me in case you have any questions, and I will do my best to answer. For things like — payments, coverage decisions, policy questions — Marissa, your desk adjuster is the best point of contact."

Emily took the card with a small, grateful smile.

"Thanks for explaining all that."

"No problem," he said. "It's part of the job. The last thing I will say is typically coverage decisions are made within 7-10 business days. Sometimes they are shorter or longer, but this is the standard I'm required to tell everyone.

You should get in contact with that mitigation company as soon as I head out as well. Oh, one more major thing. For all the contents of your home you should make a list that describes the objects you've purchased, how much you purchased it for and how old they are."

"What are contents?"

"Contents are items not fixed to the home. Like beds/bedframes, couches or tv's."

"I see," Emily jotted this down in her phone.

"Once you've compiled this list please email it to Marissa. She'll be able to refer it to the contents division who will handle pricing. I've taken pictures of the damaged contents I saw in the different rooms, so they'll have pictures as well. Any other questions before I go?"

"Not right now but I'll call if anything. Thanks."

"No problem. Thanks, and talk soon."

Ryan headed out the door. Emily closed it, and leaned back against it.

So far, the process hadn't been as terrifying as she'd feared.

But she also knew this was just the beginning.

Over the next few days, the real work — and the real battle for fair coverage — would start.

CHAPTER 3

Mitigation At Its Finest

After meeting with Ryan, Emily called the mitigation company Marissa recommended. By noon the next day, the mitigation crew arrived.

"Morning!" said the lead tech, Tony. "We're here to get the place drying out."

Emily led them inside, explaining that the insurance adjuster had already inspected.

"Good," Tony said, unpacking his moisture meter. "That saves time. We'll take some baseline readings, set up equipment, and get this house stabilized."

Two men in blue polo shirts and heavy boots lugged industrial fans, dehumidifiers, and moisture meters throughout Emily's house. The truck parked in her driveway had a giant logo: **Rapid Recovery Restoration.**

First, the walkthrough.

Emily repeated the steps she took with Ryan with Tony. First showing the cause of the damage and bringing him through each of the damaged rooms. Unlike Ryan, Tony began taking readings and jotting down notes of each room they walked through.

Tony poked the moisture meter against the swollen drywall. It beeped angrily. The numbers on the screen flashed red.

"Ceilings still saturated," he said.
He pressed the meter against the floorboards — same thing.

He moved systematically through each room. Even the walls Emily thought looked dry were wet behind the drywall exterior.

"You can't always see water damage right away," Tony explained. "It wicks inside walls and under floors. If we don't dry it properly now, you'll have mold in a few weeks."

Emily's stomach tightened. She's heard so many horror stories about mold growing up she was nervous at the mention.

Next, the emergency plan.

Tony outlined the immediate steps:

- **Remove** soaked carpets and padding.
- **Tear out** heavily saturated drywall sections ("flood cuts" about two feet up from the floor).
- **Pull up** any vinyl and hardwood flooring that was too wet to save.
- **Assess** the subfloor after flooring is removed.
- **Set up industrial fans and dehumidifiers** to dry the studs, subfloor, and open cavities.

"This is considered 'emergency mitigation,'" Tony said. "It's standard practice after a water loss. Your insurance should cover it — minus your deductible."

He handed Emily a form titled **Work Authorization and Assignment of Benefits**.

It allowed Rapid Recovery to start work immediately and authorized them to bill her insurance company directly.

Emily paused.
She remembered something Marissa had said:

"You're responsible for vetting vendors. We can recommend, but we don't guarantee payment for whatever they charge."

She read the fine print carefully.
The form gave the company the right to pursue payment from insurance — but if insurance didn't pay enough, Emily could be stuck covering the difference.

KEY TIP

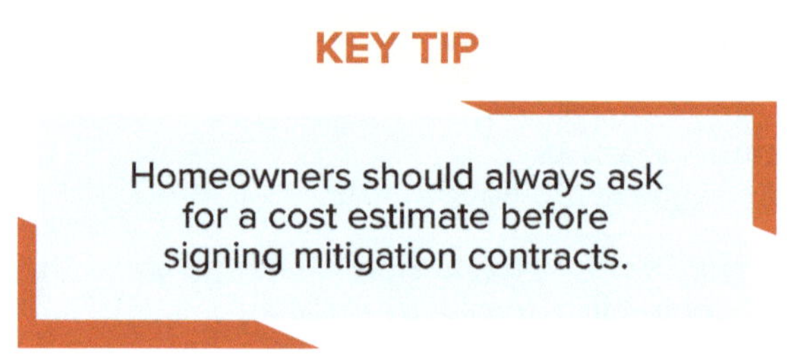

"I'll sign," Emily said, "but first, can you give me a rough idea of what this will cost?"

Tony nodded.

"For this level of water loss? Probably between $6,000 and $9,000. Depends how long it takes to dry and how much needs to be removed. We'll give you the same itemized bill for everything that we'll send to the insurance but the faster we work the faster we can avoid further damage."

He explained that insurance companies typically used a standardized pricing program called **Xactimate**, which Rapid Recovery followed closely.

Feeling slightly reassured, Emily signed.

The crew immediately started setting up — pulling up ruined carpet, slicing into swollen drywall, positioning noisy fans in strategic corners.

The next morning, Marissa called.

"Hi Emily, I have your preliminary estimate from Ryan's inspection."

Emily switched her phone to speaker mode and opened her laptop to take notes.

Marissa explained:

- The **estimate** totaled $42,400 for covered repairs (including drywall replacement, flooring removal, and repainting).
- Her **deductible** — $1,500 — was already subtracted from the amount that was listed on the estimate.
- **Emergency mitigation** costs were still **pending** because they hadn't been invoiced yet.

"And remember," Marissa said, "this is an initial estimate. If the mitigation team finds additional hidden damage, we can reopen the claim and reassess. They'll send us an itemized bill along with pictures for that process."

Emily clicked open the email Marissa sent.
It contained a 32-page document — the estimate in mind-numbing detail, categorized each room and listed things like:

- "Remove & Replace 5/8" drywall"
- "Detaching and resetting light fixtures"
- "Content manipulation (moving furniture)"

It also listed **depreciation amounts** for some items — meaning she would only be paid their "actual cash value" until repairs were completed and confirmed by the contractor.

KEY TIP

Homeowners often get paid in two stages — partial payment now, and "recoverable depreciation" later, after proof repairs are made. If contractors disagree with the payment, they should write estimates that also detail the additional costs of the repair. These estimates should be as itemized as possible, with the costs of material and labor as separate costs. A lump sum is unable to be assessed properly and can delay the process.

The first problem arose immediately after reviewing the document.

Emily scrolled and realized that her upstairs bathroom — the source of the leak — wasn't fully addressed in the scope. At least not from the damage the mitigation company assessed.

Only a small patch of drywall was listed for repair.

She called Marissa back.

"Shouldn't the bathroom flooring and maybe the subfloor be included too?" she asked.

"Good catch," Marissa said. "We base estimates on visible damage. If the mitigation company finds more damage — like water trapped under tiles or mold — they can submit a supplement request."

Marissa explained how **supplemental claims** worked:

- Contractors document the extra damage.
- The insurance company reviews estimates and, if justified, may approve additional payments.

Emily wrote it all down in her claim log.

That night, sitting cross-legged in her hotel bed, Emily reviewed everything:

- Claim number and contacts. ✓
- Water mitigation authorized and started. ✓
- Preliminary insurance estimate received. ✓
- Supplement likely needed. ✓

She realized that while things were moving, she would have to be her own best advocate.

This wasn't just about filing paperwork anymore.

It was about managing a recovery project, step by step, on her own home.

CHAPTER 4

Reading the Fine Print

Three days later, Emily's house sounded like a small airplane hangar and felt like a sauna.

The mitigation fans roared day and night, rattling the walls and making normal conversation nearly impossible without shouting. The entire first floor was stripped down to bare studs. Upstairs, all the rooms had at least 2' of drywall cut revealing the beam. The flooring was removed everywhere, except the bathrooms, revealing only the subfloor. The bathroom, which caused all of this, floor felt shifty underfoot — a bad sign.

Tony from Rapid Recovery stopped by that morning with a clipboard.

"We need to talk," a serious, heavy tone in his voice.

Emily set down her coffee and followed him through the house. They made their way up to the master bathroom. The culprit in all this damage.

"There's water under your tiles," Tony said, as he pointed to the corner of the ceramic tiles with a gloved hand. "The subfloors saturated and dipped ever so slightly when walked on. It smells like early-stage mold growth too."

"We need to pull the bathroom flooring, treat the subfloor, and maybe replace sections if they turn out to be rotten."

Emily nodded. "Okay. Was that in the original insurance estimate?"

Tony shook his head.

"This would be a **supplement**. We'll need to submit photos, a revised estimate, and ask your insurer for additional funds to continue."

Understanding Supplements

That afternoon, Tony's office emailed Marissa and CC'd Emily with a
Supplement Request Form — complete with:

- Photos of the hidden water damage.
- A revised scope of work which included the new findings.
- A detailed cost estimate for the additional repairs (about $5,000).

Emily reviewed it carefully.
She realized this supplement included more than just pulling up floors — it
called for **mold treatment**, **new underlayment**, and **retiling** the bathroom.

Marissa called the next business day.

"Hi Emily. How are you?"

"Wish things were better. Did you get a chance to look at the documents Rapid
Recovery emailed?" there was a pinch of worry and defeat in her voice.

"Yes, I have and that's what I wanted to discuss. I received the supplement
Rapid Recovery submitted," she said. "We'll review it. Keep in mind, some items
— like mold remediation — are limited by your policy."

Emily sat up straighter.

"Wait, limited how?"

"Your policy has a $10,000 mitigation cap, and certain procedures like mold
remediation require additional endorsements on your insurance policy. I'll
double check to see if this is included and we can assess the additional
monetary approval needed regarding this," Marissa explained. "Depending on
the situation, some items might not be fully reimbursed. We will allow for Rapid
Recovery to begin the process but please keep in mind this limit."

First Friction

Two days later, the claims department sent Emily a **Partial Approval Letter** via
email.
It agreed to pay for:

- Subfloor replacement.
- New underlayment.
- Bathroom retiling.

BUT they denied:

- Full mold remediation costs ("no mold endorsement").
- Emergency antimicrobial treatments the mitigation company applied before insurer approval.

The insurance offer was about **$2,800 less** than the supplement requested. Tony wasn't happy when he heard.

"They're trying to nickel and dime you," he muttered over the phone. "We did what we had to do to prevent worse damage."

Emily felt caught in the middle.
Rapid Recovery expected payment in full — either from the insurance or from her.

She called Marissa again, this time determined to push back.

"I understand the mold cap," Emily said calmly, "but the emergency antimicrobial spray was part of mitigation to prevent further damage. Isn't that covered under emergency services?"

There was a long pause on the line.

"You make a good point," Marissa finally said. "Let me escalate this to my supervisor."

Standing Her Ground

Two days after that, Emily received an updated payment offer:
The insurance company agreed to cover an **additional $1,800** for the antimicrobial treatment as part of emergency mitigation — still leaving a small gap but much closer to the real cost.

It wasn't a perfect win, but it was a reminder:
Speaking up mattered.

Had Emily accepted the first denial quietly; she would have been left covering hundreds — maybe thousands — of dollars herself.

She updated her claim log:

- Date of supplement request. ✓
- Scope of supplement. ✓
- Original approval and denial. ✓
- Appeal and final adjustment. ✓

<h1 style="text-align:center">KEY LESSON</h1>

Insurance companies can sometimes underpay on initial estimates. They are only to assess the damage that is present and not remove anything. The supplement process is necessary when there are additional damages the adjuster couldn't see are revealed. Persistence — and specific, documented challenges — often lead to better outcomes.

Considering Help

Later that night, Emily found herself Googling:

"What does a public adjuster do?"

She learned that **public adjusters** represented homeowners — not insurance companies — and could help negotiate claims, especially if the insurer dragged its feet or kept underpaying.

Some charged flat fees; others took a percentage of the claim payout (usually 10–15% of the final payment).

Emily decided to keep going on her own for now. But she saved the names of two licensed public adjusters nearby — her own little insurance policy.

By the end of the week, Emily had:

- A **revised insurance estimate** reflecting the supplement.
- **Approval** for emergency mitigation costs.
- **Partial mold remediation** coverage up to her policy limit (as this would include the removal of the wet subfloor not a mold treatment).
- A clear timeline to **start permanent repairs.**

The battle wasn't over.

But for the first time in days, she felt like she was winning. The victories were small, but they were still meaningful.

CHAPTER 5

Dealing with Contractors

With the supplement approved and the mitigation fans finally silenced; Emily faced her next challenge:

Choosing a contractor.

Rapid Recovery offered to handle the full rebuild, but Emily wanted at least one other bid. Just to be safe. She'd heard too many horror stories about insurance repairs going sideways when homeowners rushed into contracts, and she wanted to have as many perspectives as possible.

KEY TIP

Always get at least two estimates — even if the insurance company recommends someone. It will allow you to assess the costs of repairs better. Also keep in mind that these contractors should be licensed and insured. It is your choice to use someone who isn't, but licensed and insured is always recommended by insurance companies.

The Search

She posted a request on a local community app, and within a day, two independent contractors responded.

After scheduling walk-throughs, Emily met with both.

Both contractors agreed:

- The upstairs bathroom required gutting and rebuilding — new subfloor, new tile, new vanity.
- Drywall and flooring needed to be replaced in the bedrooms and closets.
- Extensive drywall and insulation work was needed throughout the first floor, with possible rewiring after an electrician's assessment.
- Flooring had to be replaced throughout the living room, dining room, hallway, stairs and kitchen.
- Basement needed to be cleaned. Preferably pressure washed on the concrete.

Each contractor promised to "work with insurance pricing," but Emily quickly realized that meant **different things**.

Contractor A (Steve's Restoration):

- Promised to "waive" her deductible — which sounded tempting but felt shady. What was that supposed to mean anyways.
- Handed Emily a one-page agreement with little detail.
- Had a lump sum estimate which had general details of work needed.

Contractor B (Summit Builders):

- Provided an overall scope of work detailing how many rooms needed repair and work needed in each one.
- Provided a line-by-line estimate which detailed material and labor costs separately.
- Explained the "supplement path" if hidden damage popped up during repairs.
- Required a signed agreement **and** contact information for the desk adjuster in case any issues arose.

Choosing Wisely

Emily remembered the advice she had read during her late-night research:

"If a contractor offers to 'eat' your deductible, it's a red flag — often leading to corner-cutting or insurance fraud issues."

With that quote ringing in her ears, she chose **Summit Builders**, even though they weren't the cheapest.

When the project manager, Carlos, sent over the **construction agreement**, Emily spent two hours reading it carefully.

She spotted a few terms she needed to understand:

- **Insurance Proceeds Clause**: Payment would come from whatever the insurance company paid — plus any approved supplements.
- **Holdback Acknowledgment**: She was responsible for covering any **depreciation holdbacks** until final repairs were verified.
- **Change Order Policy**: If she decided to upgrade materials (like fancier flooring), she'd owe the difference — not insurance.

Carlos patiently explained:

"Your insurance claim will release payments in phases. Usually, you get an initial check, then after we finish and submit final photos and invoices, you get the **recoverable depreciation** amount."

Emily highlighted that in her notes.

Holdbacks and Recoverable Depreciation

The insurance company had already paid her the **Actual Cash Value (ACV)** of the damaged materials — meaning the value after "wear and tear" deductions.

They were **holding back** about $5,500 — the **depreciation** — until Emily completed repairs and proved she spent the money on actual restoration.

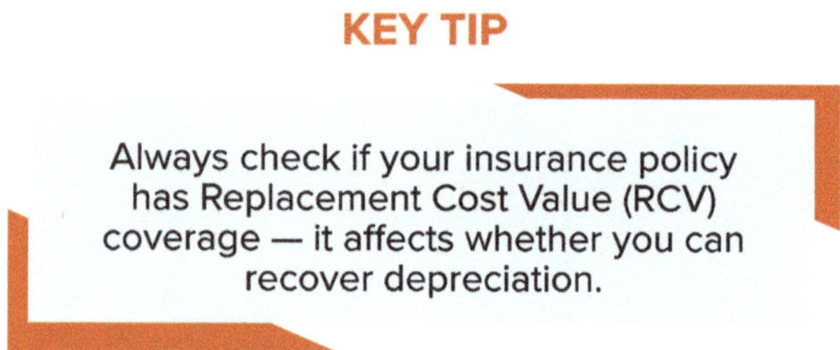

Carlos promised to help her submit the **Certificate of Completion** once the repairs were finished. But he warned her:

"If you don't fix everything listed in the estimate, or if you do cheaper work, the insurance company might reduce or deny some of the holdback."

Emily gulped. It wasn't just about getting the work done — it had to be documented and matched to the original scope or better if the original could not be achieved.

Final Preparations

Emily signed Summit Builders' contract — with handwritten notes added, making it crystal clear:

- No work changes without her written approval.
- Any supplements would be reviewed by her before submission.

Repairs were scheduled to start in a week.

Before the crew arrived, Emily:

- Photographed the entire house again. Documenting everything the mitigation had removed and areas they pointed out while doing
- their final check walkthrough. ✓
- Backed up all insurance emails and documents into cloud storage. ✓
- Labeled all insurance checks separately in her bank account. ✓

She felt like a project manager now, not just a homeowner.

By all accounts it wasn't a glamorous position. It was a smart one. This is when she finally understood:

The claim wasn't truly over until the house was rebuilt — and the last insurance dollar recovered.

CHAPTER 6

Surprises and Setbacks

At 7:00 a.m. sharp on Monday morning, Emily's driveway filled with trucks.

The Summit Builders crew poured in — tool belts jangling, coffee in hand, ready to start what Carlos had promised would be a **four-week rebuild**.

The first day was noisy but encouraging.

Huge rolls of insulation were set up for installation. New subfloor panels were nailed down. New drywall brought in. Materials for flooring and tile were dropped off neatly on the front lawn.

Emily watched from the kitchen doorway, feeling hopeful for the first time in weeks.

First Surprise: Building Permits

That afternoon, Carlos tapped gently on her front door.

"Hey, quick thing," he said. "We need to pull a building permit for the bathroom subfloor and tile work. City code requires it."

Emily blinked.

"I thought the insurance estimate already covered everything?"

Carlos shook his head.

"Insurance pays for the repairs but **permits and inspections are separate**. Some policies reimburse permit fees, but you'll need to pay upfront."

The permit would cost around **$300**.

Emily sighed but agreed. Carlos promised to add it to the supplement request for the insurance to review later.

KEY TIP

Homeowners should clarify early whether permit fees are covered — and keep all receipts to submit for reimbursement if the payment is not made immediately. They should also ensure they have code upgrades coverage. In the declarations page this is referred to as Ordinance and Law coverage.

Second Surprise: Material Shortages

A few days later, as workers lay down fresh subflooring in the living room, Carlos approached Emily again.

"Hey, there's a delay on the flooring you picked out," he said. "Supply chain issues. We can wait two weeks … or use a very similar product available now. The major difference between the two is price."

He handed her two sample planks.

The alternative looked almost identical but cost about **$1.50 more per square foot**. The slight thickness of the more expensive one must've been the reason.

Insurance had priced the floor at $5.00/sq ft in the original estimate. The replacement would push the material cost to **$6.50/sq ft** — an out-of-pocket cost for Emily.

She had a choice:

- Wait, delaying the completion of the project.
- Eat the difference in price and continue with repairs as scheduled.
- Or fight the insurance company for a price increase (with no guarantee).

Emily chose to wait.

The old her — the impatient one — might have thrown money at the problem. The new Emily was committed to managing the claim **smartly**, not emotionally.

If material upgrades are optional (not required), insurance usually won't pay the difference. Stay within the approved scope unless otherwise necessary. This again is where Ordinance and Law coverage comes into play. If an upgrade is required based on codes by the city, county, or state you live in, this coverage will kick in to help mitigate the difference in costs. Assuming you have this coverage. If you don't, unfortunately, you'll have to eat those costs.

Third Surprise: Inspection Fail

Two weeks in, the city inspector arrived to sign off on the subfloor and rough plumbing work.

Emily hovered nearby, pretending to check her emails.

The inspector frowned at something.

"Who installed these P-traps?" he asked, pointing to the bathroom sink drains. "Our plumber," Carlos said.

"These are the wrong material for code in this district. You'll need to swap them before I can pass this stage."

Carlos apologized and promised to fix it immediately.

But Emily made a mental note:
Even trusted contractors could make mistakes — and **city inspections** protected *her*, not just the bureaucracy.

Always welcome city inspections during rebuilds. They can catch problems that protect homeowners from future legal and safety issues. Just another reminder that Ordinance and Law coverage will come in handy. We can't stress this enough. Older homes may have codes that were grandfathered in and when repairs are being made will need to be upgraded.

Dealing with Supplements During Repairs

While waiting for permit re-inspections, Carlos submitted a small **supplement** to Emily's desk adjuster:

- $300 permit fee.
- Additional labor costs for the code regulations regarding plumbing.

Emily received a notice from the insurance company requesting:

- A copy of the permit invoice.
- Before-and-after photos.
- An updated contractor invoice.

She quickly uploaded everything via the insurer's online portal.

Three days later, insurance approved the supplement — issuing an additional $750 payment.

Small victories, Emily thought. Small victories.

Each tiny piece of the puzzle — supplements, documentation, inspections — committed itself to the larger picture.

The Emotional Rollercoaster

Midway through the repairs, Emily hit a wall emotionally.

The dust never seemed to settle. Her living space was cramped and chaotic. Strangers came and went, hammering, shouting, blasting radios.

One morning she woke to find a fresh gouge in her newly painted wall — careless damage caused by moving a ladder.

Carlos promised to fix it without charge, but it was a reminder:
Even good crews make mistakes.
Nothing about rebuilding was smooth.

Emily kept a growing punch-list:

- Paint touch-ups needed. ✔
- Replace the splintered baseboard. ✔

Carlos assured her that before final payment, a full **walkthrough inspection** would take place to address any areas that needed more attention.

The Finish Line Approaching

By the end of the fourth week, Emily's house looked nearly whole again.

The bathroom was pristine — new tile sparkling under the bright vanity lights.
The living room floor gleamed.
Fresh drywall and clean paint erased the worst memories of the flood.

Summit Builders scheduled a **final walkthrough** between Emily and Carlos.
She walked room by room, checking each punch-list item, marking corrections
with blue painter's tape.

Two days later, Carlos sent her:

- A **Final Invoice** matching the insurance payments.
- A **Certificate of Completion** form for insurance.
- Before-and-after photo documentation.

Emily double-checked everything, then submitted it all to her insurer.

Now, she just had to wait for the final holdback payment — the last piece of the
financial puzzle.

CHAPTER 7

Closing the Claim and Life After the Leak

Emily could hardly believe it.

After six chaotic weeks of mitigation, arguments, paperwork, and construction noise, her home was finally whole again.

There was just one last hurdle:
Closing out the insurance claim properly.

Submitting the Certificate of Completion

Following Carlos' instructions, Emily:

- Signed the **Certificate of Completion.**
- Attached the contractor's **final invoice.**
- Uploaded detailed **before-and-after photos** of all repairs.

She sent the full packet to Marissa, her assigned desk adjuster, along with a short, professional email:

"Dear Marissa, attached is the documentation verifying repairs are complete. Please advise regarding the release of recoverable depreciation. Thank you!"

Now she waited.

Understanding the Final Payment

A few days later, Emily received an email with good news:

*"Based on your submitted documentation, we have approved the release of
the recoverable depreciation amount of $5,536.00.
Payment will be mailed within 7–10 business days."*

Emily did a little fist-pump at her kitchen counter.

She had **earned** this final check — not just with repairs, but by **managing the claim smartly** at every step.

KEY TIP

Depreciation is usually only reimbursed if:
- The repairs match the insurer's approved scope.
- All work is completed professionally.
- Final invoices and evidence are submitted properly.

Missing a step could have cost her thousands. Around $5,536.00 to be exact.

Handling Final Contractor Payment

Carlos had already received insurance payments for completed stages of work, but Emily owed him one final amount — the **recoverable depreciation** portion.

They had an upfront agreement that once she received the final insurance payment, she would pay Summit Builders.

Emily deposited the $5,536.00 insurance check the day it arrived.
She transferred the exact amount to Summit Builders' account electronically — efficiency was a priority.

Carlos emailed her a paid-in-full receipt, a warranty certificate covering workmanship for **five years**, and a lien waver stating they won't place a lien on the property as work is the work has been paid for.

Emily filed everything neatly, just in case she ever needed to revisit this mess:

- Contractor contract.
- Paid invoices.
- Warranty documents.
- Insurance payment summaries.

Official Claim Closure

A week later, Emily received the final letter from her insurance company:

"Your claim is now considered closed. If you discover any additional damage related to this loss within 12 months, you may request a supplemental review."

It felt surreal.
For weeks, managing the claim had consumed her free time, her patience, even her sleep. Thoughts of worry and impatience riddled her mind. Now, with one email, it was officially **finished**.

Emily sat back, surveying her fresh floors, her sparkling bathroom, her clean drywall.

The journey hadn't been perfect. There were mistakes, frustrations, and close calls. But she realized something important:

She was no longer just a homeowner.
She was a **homeowner who understood her insurance rights**.

The Final Lessons

Before closing her notebook, Emily wrote down five lessons she didn't want to forget:

1. **Document Everything:** Photos, calls, contracts — every piece mattered.
2. **Understand Your Policy:** Coverage details can make or break a claim.
3. **Speak Up Early:** Denials aren't always final; smart appeals can work.
4. **Manage Your Contractor:** Supervise the rebuilding as your own project manager.
5. **Stay Patient:** Claims are marathons, not sprints.

These lessons wouldn't just help her someday if disaster struck again. They might help friends, neighbors — even complete strangers. Because knowledge wasn't just power.

It was protection.

Homeowner Survival Tip: Your Insurance Binder

Every homeowner should have a simple "Insurance Binder" ready long before a disaster.

Yours should include:

- A full copy of your current insurance policy.
- Copies of recent home inspections.
- Photos/videos of all major belongings (inventory).
- Contact information for your insurance agent, preferred contractors, and emergency services.
- Claim action checklist.

Store it physically (fireproof safe!) **and digitally** (cloud storage, encrypted flash drive).

Prepared homeowners settle faster, fight smarter, and sleep easier.

EPILOGUE

The Water Is Gone, But Something Remains

The fans, the plastic sheeting, the soggy chaos — all of it, gone.

The floors were dry. The walls were painted. It was like a whole new home.

Emily stood in the doorway of her bathroom, the one that had caused all the trouble, and took in the familiar room with unfamiliar eyes. The new vanity was a close match to the old one. The drywall was smooth, freshly painted, no longer bubbling or bruised. And the floors... she almost didn't recognize them. They gleamed now.

You wouldn't know if a loss had ever happened here.

But she did.

Not just because of the photos she kept in a digital folder labeled *"Plumbing Claim - 2025"*, the emails between her and the adjusters, or the dry log that still sat in her inbox. No — she knew because the experience changed her. Not drastically. Not painfully. But definitively.

■ A Crash Course She Never Asked For

Before the leak, insurance was a checkbox on a list of monthly bills.

Now? It was a world of terms, people, decisions, and quiet dependencies.

Emily learned what a mitigation company did — and what they didn't do. She learned that estimates weren't always final, that not all damage is visible at first, and that just because she has insurance doesn't mean any and everything is automatically covered. She learned to ask questions. The right ones.

And she learned that, sometimes, the most important people in a claim aren't the ones who write the checks — they're the ones who show up. The adjuster with the tablet. The crew that worked through the night. The people who answered her emails when she wasn't sure if she'd done something wrong.

■ More Than a Repair

Emily never wanted to become "experienced" at filing a claim. If there was one thing, she'd tell the version of herself standing at the front door on the day she got home from vacation, it would be this:

You're going to get through this. And no, you don't have to know everything today. Document everything. Ask those obvious questions.
And above all... be kind to yourself. This is a process.

The water was gone. The insurance claim was over.

But one thing stayed.

Confidence.

CHAPTER GUIDE

Chapter By Chapter Steps Every Homeowner Should Take

CHAPTER 1

Stage: Discovery of Loss & Initial Reaction

Act Fast, Document Everything
When you discover major damage, immediately:

- Take **photos/videos** before cleanup starts.
- Preventing further damage (e.g., shut off water when there is a leak.).
- **Don't discard** damaged items yet — they may be needed for inspection.
- **Call your insurance carrier's 24/7 line**, not just your agent.
- This first 24 hours sets the tone for the entire claim.

File Clean, File Clear
When filing your claim:

- Write down your **claim number** and both of your assigned adjusters' name/contact info.
- Be clear but calm in your description of the damage (no exaggeration).
- Ask for the next steps and documentation requirements.
- Note all conversations in your own **claim logbook.** Your job now is to create a paper trail that protects you later.

📍 *Stage: Meeting the Adjuster*

Make Your Home "Inspection Ready"
The field adjuster's inspection is critical. Help it go smoothly:

- Have all areas accessible and safe to walk through (as much as possible).
- Mention hidden damage they might miss (wet subfloors, smells, mold, etc.).
- Walk with them and take **your own notes/photos.**
- Ask when you'll receive the adjuster's **estimate.**
- You only get one first impression — make it count.

CHAPTER 3

📍 *Stage: Mitigation Begins*

Don't Just Watch — Manage the Mitigation Crew
Mitigation companies move fast — sometimes too fast.

- **Take photos of everything** before and after demolition.
- Ask for a **written scope of work** and itemized equipment list.
- Monitor for over-drying or unnecessary demolition.
- Don't assume your insurance will cover everything they do.
- Always keep the adjuster informed of major mitigation actions.

CHAPTER 4

📍 *Stage: Reviewing the Estimate & First Payment*

Know What You're Owed
Understand the terms behind your payment:

- **ACV (Actual Cash Value)** = depreciated payout.
- **RCV (Replacement Cost Value)** = full value if you repair.
- **Deductible** is subtracted from your payment. (i.e. if your deductible is $1,000.00 and your approved payment is $10,000.00 for your claim, you will only receive $9,000.00)

- Review the estimate line-by-line for missing items.
- If you disagree, you can request a **revised scope** or even a reinspection. A contractor estimate with details about additional or missing repair items will help your case.

CHAPTER 5

♀ *Stage: Hiring Contractors & Starting Rebuild*

Choose the Right Contractor — Not Just the Fastest One
Vet your rebuild team like you're hiring for a job, because you are:

- Require a **written contract** with scope, timeline, and payment terms.
- Never pay 100% up front — use milestone payments. (i.e. partial payment upfront is standard practice and then final payment upon completion.)
- Confirm your insurer approves their scope before work begins.
- Watch out for **"scope creep"** that your policy won't cover.
- The contractor is your partner — but you're still the project manager.

CHAPTER 5

♀ *Stage: Finalizing the Claim*

Don't Leave Money on the Table
Before closing your claim:

- Submit **proof of completed work** to the insurance company (photos, invoices, signed certificate).
- Request release of **recoverable depreciation.**
- Get **warranty documents** and lien waivers from contractors. (i.e. this gives a guarantee that the work is completed and paid for, and the contractor cannot place a lien on your home for non-payment.)
- Ask for a final **"claim closed"** confirmation from your insurer.
- The end of repairs doesn't mean your claim is over — until *you* confirm it is.

CHAPTER 7

♀ *Stage: After the Claim — Preparing for the Future*

Turn Experience into Preparedness
Now that you've been through it, don't just move on — level up:

- Build a **home inventory** (video + receipts).
- Review your **policy limits** and coverage gaps.
- Make a one-page **claim checklist** for future emergencies.
- Save contacts for **trusted vendors.**
- Being prepared once means you'll never be caught off guard again.

APPENDIX A

Appendix A: Sample Checklist

Emergency Claim Response Checklist
Do this immediately after discovering damage:

- ☐ Ensure safety (shut off water/electric/gas if needed)

- ☐ Take clear photos/videos of all damage **before cleaning up**

- ☐ Prevent further damage (e.g., place buckets, towels, tarps)

- ☐ Contact insurance carrier's **24/7 claims line**

- ☐ Start a **claim journal**: dates, names, phone numbers

- ☐ Locate your insurance policy and review coverage

- ☐ Do not throw anything away before the adjuster sees it. (If you do have pictures of the debris for the adjuster to include in their report)

- ☐ Call a reputable **mitigation company**, ask insurer if they have one they work with. (For water damage related claims.)

Claim Management Checklist
Stay organized during the process:

- [ ] Maintain a physical or digital claim folder for your records.
- [ ] Save all emails, texts, voicemails, and documents associated with your claim.
- [ ] Document every conversation with the adjusters and contractors
- [ ] Request all estimates and payment breakdowns in writing
- [ ] Confirm approvals before making repairs
- [ ] Track payments (ACV, RCV, depreciation) and deductibles
- [ ] Monitor contractor work and keep before/after photos
- [ ] Ask contractor for final walkthrough upon repair completion

Homeowner Preparedness Checklist
Use before disaster ever happens:

- [ ] Create a **photo/video inventory** of home and belongings (mainly major purchases or things of sentimental value)
- [ ] Store receipts for major purchases
- [ ] Review insurance policy annually (coverage, deductibles, exclusions)
- [ ] Know your carrier's claim hotline and your policy number
- [ ] Save contacts for trusted vendors: contractors, plumbers, electricians, mitigation company
- [ ] Keep a printed **Claim Action Plan** in your emergency binder
- [ ] Digitally back up all documents (cloud or encrypted drive)

APPENDIX B

Appendix B: Glossary Of Insurance Terms

Actual Cash Value (ACV) – The depreciated value of an item or repair. What your insurer pays before deducting depreciation.

Additional Living Expenses (ALE) – Coverage that helps pay for temporary housing and meals if your home is uninhabitable.

Approval – A coverage determination in which payment will be made in relation to covered perils under policy limits.

Contents – Items the insured has purchased that are not attached to the dwelling. (i.e. tv's, computers, bedding etc.)

Denial – A coverage determination in which no payment will be made due to policy exclusion or lack of qualifying damage.

Deductible – The amount the policyholder "pays out of pocket" on a claim before insurance coverage begins. (Note this is applied to the estimate you receive and is not a new expense.)

Depreciation – The loss in value over time due to age, wear, or obsolescence.

Desk Adjuster – A licensed adjuster hired by the insurance company who will make the final determination on coverage. They have the full policy on hand and will approve any estimates and final payments the field adjuster recommends, based on the policy limits.

Exclusion – A condition or item that is not covered under the policy.

Endorsement (or Rider) – An optional addition to an insurance policy that adds or modifies coverage.

Field Adjuster – A licensed independent adjuster who will do an in-person inspection of the damage you reported. They often do not work directly for the insurance company and cannot make a coverage decision.

Lien Waiver – A document from a contractor confirming they've been paid and will not file a lien on your property.

Mitigation – Immediate efforts to prevent further damage after a loss (e.g., water removal, drying).

Overhead & Profit (O&P) – Additional percentage in estimates reflecting contractor coordination and supervision, typically applied to complex or multi-trade jobs.

Public Adjuster – A licensed independent adjuster hired by the policyholder to represent them in a claim.

Recoverable Depreciation – The portion of ACV held back by the insurer until you submit proof that repairs or replacements have been completed.

Replacement Cost Value (RCV) – The full cost to replace an item with new materials of similar kind and quality.

Scope of Loss – A detailed breakdown of what was damaged and what it will cost to repair or replace.

Subrogation – When your insurer seeks reimbursement from a third party responsible for the loss. (i.e. if the water heater leaked and the damage was caused by a faulty manufacturer part, the insurance will seek reimbursement from the manufacturer)

Supplement – Additional payment request submitted post-inspection due to newly discovered or previously omitted items.

Resources and Further Reading

- **Claim It: Debunked Homeowner's Insurance Myths** for common misunderstandings people may have about homeowner's insurance.

- **Claim It: The Homeowner's Workbook** for fillable checklists and claim documentation examples.

- **Claim It: An Adjuster's POV** for a look at what field adjusters do and how they handle claims.

- NAIC: National Association of Insurance Commissioners
- Insurance Information Institute
- FEMA Flood Resources
- Consumer Financial Protection Bureau
- **Digital Home Inventory Apps:**
    - Sortly
    - Encircle
    - Nest Egg
    - Google Sheets or Excel (manual option)
- Ready.gov Disaster Preparedness Toolkit
- Sample Scope of Loss Templates (varies by state – search "[State] scope of loss PDF")

www.ingramcontent.com/pod-product-compliance
Lightning Source LLC
Chambersburg PA
CBHW061032100726
47911CB00006B/165